HOW I SURVIVED MIDDLE SCHOOL

Cheat Sheet

Check out these other books in the
How I Survived Middle School series by Nancy Krulik:

Can You Get an F in Lunch?

Madame President

I Heard a Rumor

The New Girl

HOW I SURVIVED MIDDLE SCHOOL

Cheat Sheet

By Nancy Krulik

SCHOLASTIC INC.

New York   Toronto   London   Auckland   Sydney
Mexico City   New Delhi   Hong Kong   Buenos Aires

No part of this publication may be reproduced, stored in a retrieval system, or transmitted in any form or by any means, electronic, mechanical, photocopying, recording, or otherwise, without written permission of the publisher. For information regarding permission, write to Scholastic Inc., Attention: Permissions Department, 557 Broadway, New York, NY 10012.

ISBN-13: 978-0-545-01304-8
ISBN-10: 0-545-01304-6

Copyright © 2007 by Nancy Krulik

Published by Scholastic Inc. All rights reserved.
SCHOLASTIC and associated logos are trademarks and/or registered trademarks of Scholastic Inc.

12 11 10 9 8   9 10 11 12/0

Printed in the U.S.A.   40
First printing, October 2007
Book design by Alison Klapthor

For my Sarah and Emily, my middle school muses

What Kind of Rock Star are You?

Are you a heavy metal monster who rocks the school, or a hip-hop honey who tells it like it is? Is finding harmony your specialty, or do you march to a different drummer? To find out where you fall on the musical *scale,* take this quickie quiz.

1. **When you walk into a bookstore, what type of book do you typically choose?**

   A. A romance novel
   B. A quirky comedy
   C. An action adventure
   D. A fantasy novel or a comic book

2. If you could have any pet in the whole world, which would you bring home?

A. A soft kitten
B. A ferret
C. A chatty parakeet
D. An energetic puppy

3. Your favorite type of music is:

A. Soft and soothing
B. Upbeat and good for dancing
C. Loud and fast
D. Rhythmic and fun

4. What's your favorite way to spend a Saturday?

A. Curled up with a good book
B. Finding bargains at a flea market
C. Shooting hoops
D. Going to the movies to see a comedy

5. Your favorite outfit is best described as:

A. Warm and soft, in gentle pastel colors
B. A mix of vintage pieces you picked up at the local thrift shop
C. Athletic wear
D. Brightly colored, to make sure you stand out in the crowd

Okay, so what kind of band would you front? Total up your score to find out!

Mostly A's: You're a classical musician who puts a major focus on harmony. That's why you're the go-to girl when your friends need someone to negotiate the peace. You're a dreamer and proud of it — as you should be. Your sensitivity is your strong point, and that's a beautiful trait.

Mostly B's: Hello, pop star! You have a sense of fun that can't be beat. That genuine joy is what draws people to you. Lucky you! Your charisma will surely lead you to success.

Mostly C's: You are a true heavy metal mama. As the wild child of the band, life is one big adventure; the more exciting, the better! Your spontaneity and faith in your own style is what makes you special.

Mostly D's: Hey there, hip-hop honey! Like any good rap star, you tell it like it is, but you never go out of your way to hurt anyone. In fact, your goal in life is to share your joyous rhythm with your pals. Your friends look to you when they want the truth from someone they trust. And you never disappoint!

ONE

"DON'T FORGET TO GIVE ME YOUR INITIAL NECKLACE," my friend Marilyn reminded her twin sister, Carolyn. She handed Carolyn a delicate silver chain with a small letter M hanging from it. "Here's mine."

"Good thing you remembered," Carolyn told Marilyn as she handed her sister her necklace with the letter C on it. "That's where we got caught last time."

I watched in amazement as the twins swapped shirts, sneakers, and necklaces in the girls' room during lunch period. They really had the whole twin-switch thing down to a science.

Actually, the reason for the twins' identity swap wasn't science, but math. Carolyn was terrible in math, but Marilyn was a total numbers genius. So today, Marilyn was going to take Carolyn's math test. It was only fair, since Carolyn usually took Marilyn's Spanish tests for her.

All right, I know that's cheating. But honestly, don't most people wish they could have an identical twin or a really smart clone for situations just like this? I know I would love to have one.

However, my friend Liza had a totally different point of view. "Wouldn't it be easier for you to just study for the math test than to go through all of this?" she asked Carolyn as we watched the twins trade sneakers.

That's Liza, always the voice of reason. She's kind of like the Jiminy Cricket of our group of friends; our conscience. But that doesn't mean we always listen to her.

"No," the twins answered in one voice.

I had to laugh. In some ways Marilyn and Carolyn often seemed like the same person. They didn't just have the exact same long blond hair, bright blue eyes, and chubby cheeks. They both also seemed to know exactly what the other twin was thinking – and they usually finished each other's sentences. They said it was a twin thing. Some people found it sort of creepy. I thought it was kind of cool.

"It's just that you always forget something and get caught," Liza said. "And then you get in trouble."

Marilyn (or was it Carolyn? I wasn't sure anymore) shook her head. "Not this time. We've thought of everything. We've exchanged everything but our underwear at this point."

"That would just be gross," our friend Chloe said.

Marilyn and Carolyn laughed.

"No one is going to look that closely," Marilyn said.

"That's for sure," Carolyn agreed.

"Well I for one am completely gobsmacked," my friend Sam said. "No one will be able to tell you've changed places."

(BTW: It was okay that someone named Sam was in the girls' room with us. Sam *is* a girl. Her full name is

Samantha. And as for that whole gobsmacked thing, it's because Sam's from England. Sometimes an expression like "gobsmacked" will sneak out of her. It basically means she was really amazed.)

Just then the bathroom door swung open. Addie Wilson, Dana Harrison, and Sabrina Rosen walked in. They stood there for a minute, staring at my friends and me. The looks on their faces made it very clear that they believed we were in their territory, and we'd better get out if we knew what was good for us.

Not that the reaction was completely unexpected. The girls' bathroom in the cafeteria was pretty much accepted by everyone as the Pops' private turf.

That's what my friends and I called Addie, Dana, Sabrina, and their friends. The Pops. As in *Pop*ular. Because that was what they were: the most popular kids in the school. Not in the sense that they have more friends than anyone else. In fact, the Pops are a pretty exclusive clan. It's more that they're popular because everyone *wishes* they could be friends with them.

Every school has their own Pops. It doesn't matter what you call them – Alpha Girls, Queen Bees, Fashionistas . . . a Pop by any name is still a well-dressed, perfect-haired, makeup-loving, gossiping snob. Everyone pretty much hates them – and wants to be one of them. I can't tell you why. It's just one of those weird middle school things that defies explanation.

Most people who aren't part of the Pops' crowd just

accept their non-Pop status without question. But I think not being a Pop is even harder on me than most people, because I always sort of feel like I could have been one — *if Addie Wilson hadn't dumped me as her best friend.*

That's right. Addie Wilson — the very definition of the word Pop — had once been the friend of a mere mortal. *Me.* In fact, back when we were in elementary school, we were best friends. Inseparable. It was Addie Wilson and Jenny McAfee, BFF.

Well, make that just one F. The forever thing didn't exactly work out the way I'd planned, because the minute Addie and I first walked through the front door of Joyce Kilmer Middle School back in September, everything changed. Sometime over the summer, while I was away at overnight camp and Addie was hanging out at home, she'd decided she was too cool to be my friend any longer. Therefore our friendship was over. I hadn't had any say in the matter. So now Addie was a Pop, and I wasn't.

Not that I would ever trade my friends for phonies like Sabrina, Dana, or any of the other Pops. But deep down I have to admit that there's a part of me that wonders what it feels like to be worshipped by everyone in the school the way Addie and her friends are. I just don't let that out too often.

"Are you finished in here?" Addie huffed in my direction. "Because it's awfully crowded."

"Then maybe *you* should leave," Chloe suggested. "We were in here first. Unless of course you really have to go. . . ." She pointed to the stalls. "In which case they're all empty."

That made me laugh. Everyone knew the Pops didn't use the cafeteria girls' room as a bathroom. It was more like their clubhouse — a place to put on their makeup and gossip about everyone who wasn't a Pop — or even the Pops that weren't there. The Pops would talk behind anyone's back — even their own friends. They weren't particular.

"Let's go," Liza urged us, as she began walking toward the door. "We left Marc and Josh alone at the lunch table." Marc and Josh were two of our friends who weren't allowed in the girls' room — for obvious reasons.

"Let's see if they can figure out which of you is which," I suggested to Marilyn and Carolyn as soon as we were out of the bathroom — and out of earshot of the Pops. "It'll sort of be like a test run for your identity switch."

"Yeah," Carolyn said. "Josh is really perceptive."

"If he can't tell us apart, no one will be able to," Marilyn added.

"He won't be able to. We've made a complete identity switch," Carolyn assured her.

"From head to toe," Marilyn agreed, swinging her backpack over her shoulder. "No one will be able to tell. We're going to get away with it this time."

But I wasn't sure. "Hey, you guys," I said, pointing to their backpacks.

Marilyn and Carolyn looked at each other. Sure

enough, even though Marilyn was wearing Carolyn's clothes, she was still carrying her own backpack. And so was Carolyn.

"Oops," Marilyn said, turning her pack over to her sister.

"Good catch, Jen," Carolyn complimented me, as she handed her pack to Marilyn.

Liza shook her head. "They're gonna get caught," she insisted. "They always do."

Chapter
TWO

AS USUAL, Liza was right. At the end of the school day, I learned that the twins would be taking the late bus home along with Liza, Chloe, and me. I was staying after school for a student council meeting (I'm the sixth grade class president) and Liza was staying after school to finish up some scenery for our school play, *You're a Good Man, Charlie Brown.* Liza was too shy to ever go onstage and perform. But Chloe wasn't shy at all, which was why she was staying after school to rehearse her part in the play. She had a solo and also sang and danced in the chorus.

Marilyn and Carolyn weren't going to be having as much fun as we were, though. They were staying after school for *detention.* "What happened?" Chloe asked the twins as we walked them to the detention room. "I figured that you guys had thought of everything."

"It was all her fault!" Carolyn said, pointing to her twin.

For once, Marilyn didn't finish her sister's thought. She just sighed and looked sheepishly at her toes.

"She wrote Marilyn on top of the test paper instead of Carolyn," Carolyn continued. "How dumb is that?"

Marilyn nodded sheepishly. "I spaced out," she admitted.

"And now we have detention!" Carolyn scolded her sister.

"Forget detention." Marilyn groaned. "If you think we're in trouble here, just wait until we get home."

Carolyn looked like she was going to cry. "Mom's going to freak."

"You don't think this time she's actually going to make one of us dye our hair so our teachers can tell us apart, do you?" Marilyn asked her sister.

"You're the one who's going to have purple hair if she does," Carolyn said. "It's only fair. You're the reason we're in trouble."

"Hey! You're the one who asked me to take the test in the first place!" Marilyn reminded her.

"Yeah, well, I took your Spanish test last month," Carolyn added.

"And we got caught that time, too," Marilyn reminded her twin.

"Only because *you* answered when Jesse Nichols called you Marilyn in the hallway after class," Carolyn recalled. "You forgot you were supposed to be me!"

Okay, so now I was getting really confused. I felt like I was at a tennis match, listening as Carolyn and Marilyn bounced the blame back and forth. I was amazed that even *they* could keep track of it anymore.

Luckily, at just that moment, our friends Felicia and Rachel walked by on their way to basketball practice. "Hey,

Rachel, heard any good jokes lately?" I asked, calling them over.

Rachel looked at me with total surprise. So did everyone else. Nobody ever asks Rachel to tell one of her jokes. We don't have to. She tells them all on her own, and they're usually pretty bad.

But right now, I really wanted to change the subject before Marilyn and Carolyn got any madder at each other. And if that meant living through one of Rachel's groaners, so be it.

"Sure," Rachel said enthusiastically. "I've got a million of them." She smiled broadly. "What's big, green, fuzzy, and could hurt you if it fell out of a tree?"

"What?" I asked.

"A pool table!" Rachel exclaimed. She laughed heartily at her own joke. I joined in — not because it had been particularly funny, but to cover up for the fact that no one else was laughing. Since I'd been the one to ask her to tell the joke, I figured that was the least I could do.

"Ouch!" Felicia groaned. "Bad one, Rachel."

"Hey, Jenny asked for it," Rachel reminded her.

I sighed. "True that," I admitted. Sure the joke was bad. But at least it had stopped everyone from arguing. I didn't want everyone to start getting into it and choosing sides. The last thing I wanted was for my group of friends to start breaking off into little sub-groups. In fact, I had recently added keeping the peace in my crowd to my ever-growing list of rules they don't tell you at the sixth grade middle school orientation.

MIDDLE SCHOOL RULE #20:

DON'T FIGHT AMONGST YOURSELVES. THE BIGGER AND TIGHTER YOUR GROUP OF FRIENDS, THE BETTER. IT'S A LOT HARDER FOR OTHER KIDS TO PICK ON YOU WHEN A LOT OF PEOPLE HAVE GOT YOUR BACK.

"Anyway," Felicia said, stretching out the word to make it clear that now she was the one changing the subject, "are you guys all ready for the history test tomorrow?"

No one had to ask what history test she was asking about. For the past three or four days, the big history contest was all anyone in school had been talking about. The history challenge was a statewide contest. Every middle school student in the whole state was going to take a special history test. The kids from each county who scored the highest would then compete against one another in an even tougher history competition – a history bee at the state Capitol building.

"That's going to be one rough test," Rachel said.

At the mention of the word "test," Marilyn and Carolyn stared angrily at each other.

"You know, Joyce Kilmer Middle School has never had anyone make it to the finals of the history competition," Chloe said, entering the conversation before either of the twins could say a word. "Marc told me."

Since Marc, like Liza and the twins, was a seventh grader, I figured he would know about things like that.

"Well this year I bet we'll have at least one finalist," Felicia said. "You all know how smart Josh is."

"Of course we do," Chloe teased. "You never let us forget it."

I had to laugh at that. Josh is Felicia's boyfriend. He's practically all she talks about.

"I think Josh has a good shot at scoring high on the sixth grade test," I agreed, smiling at Felicia. Then I turned to the twins. "Do you guys think there's anyone in your grade who might win?"

Marilyn and Carolyn shrugged. "No one won last year," Marilyn began.

"So we don't have big hopes for this year," Carolyn added. "It's not like anyone in our grade suddenly became a genius."

"That's for sure," Marilyn agreed.

"I've been studying all week for the test," I told my friends. "But I know I won't get a high enough score to actually win."

"I've been studying, too," Chloe said. "I want to get a *really* high score."

"I don't know how you found the time to do that with the school play just a week away," Rachel said. "I mean you're studying all that history at the same time you're rehearsing your solo in the play, and learning all of the Lucy character's lines, too."

"Oh, it's easy," Chloe assured her. "I'm just not bothering to learn Lucy's lines."

"But aren't you the understudy for that part?" I asked her.

"Yeah, but I'm never going to get to go on stage," Chloe insisted. "The understudy only gets to go on if the real actor gets sick. And let's face it, that's never going to happen. Cassidy's never been sick or absent in the whole time she's been in middle school. She brags about it all the time."

At that moment, Cassidy walked by us on the way to the school auditorium. She was happily dancing and singing her way to rehearsal with a few other eighth graders.

"See what I mean?" Chloe asked us, sounding really disappointed. "She's totally healthy. I don't have to learn any extra lines for this play."

"Well, that'll give you more time tonight to brush up on the Revolutionary War," I said, trying to cheer her up.

"Let's not forget the Civil War," Felicia added.

"And the first Continental Congress," Rachel mentioned.

"World War I," Carolyn added.

"World War II," Marilyn said.

"The first man to land on the moon," Felicia continued.

All this history talk was beginning to make my head spin. I could tell Liza felt the same way. She seemed to be looking off into the distance, not paying much attention to the conversation.

I felt kind of bad for Liza. Our conversation had to be difficult for her. She's not a really good student. Sure, she works hard, but her grades are just okay. She didn't have a chance of doing really well on the history test, and we all knew it.

Still, Liza did have a really great talent. She was the best artist in the whole school. In fact, she was designing all the scenery for *You're a Good Man, Charlie Brown* all by herself. "How are the sets for the play looking, Liza?" I asked, trying to talk to her about something she could feel really good about.

"Better than I expected. You should see Snoopy's doghouse!" Her face brightened, and her eyes shone as she talked about her work. "I just have to put a few finishing touches on things and the whole set will be finished. And just in time, too. The show's only a week away."

"Speaking of which, I've got to get to rehearsal," Chloe said. "Come on Liza, let's go to the auditorium."

"And we'd better get to detention," Carolyn said.

"Before we're in more trouble," Marilyn added.

"I've got to get going to my meeting," I told my friends as I turned and started down the hallway. "I'll see you guys at the late buses."

Abraham Lincoln's Gettysburg Address was delivered in Gettysburg, Pennsylvania on November 19, 1863 during the Civil War, I told myself that evening as I sat at my desk and read my history book. *The Underground Railroad was a system used to bring African Americans out of slave states in the South into free states in the North.*

I could feel my eyelids getting heavy. I had a headache, too. Dates and names were all piled up in my head. I was having a tough time keeping things straight. I needed a break.

I went over to my computer and clicked on my favorite website – www.middleschoolsurvival.com. I had accidentally stumbled upon it when I was miserable and friendless after Addie dumped me for the Pops. It has articles and advice, and there are tons of quizzes about fashion and friendship. So far the quizzes on the site had helped me figure out things like whether or not Addie and I would ever be BFF again (that would be a big fat NO) and if my new friends were true blue (totally!). It also had fun quizzes that told you what cookie you're most like (I'm a vanilla sugar cookie – sweet and dependable) and whether you needed a makeover or a make*under* (my style was somewhere in the middle, which was fine with me).

"Taking a quiz will take my mind off the real test," I said aloud to my pet mice, Sam and Cody. Not that I needed to make any excuses to them. Cody and Sam would love me no matter how I scored on the history test. In fact, just the sound of my voice got them racing over to the edge of their cage so they could be nearer to me. I stuck two treats through the cage bars, just to thank them for being so loyal to me.

I glanced down at the computer screen and began navigating my way through the website. Finally I came to a quiz that totally fit.

The Stressed Test

When it comes to stress, are you a mess or do you take it all in stride? Does pressure make you ill, or are you able to just chill? To find out how you react to middle school madness, take this quickie quiz.

1. Uh-oh! Big grammar test tomorrow, and you've yet to crack a book. How do you deal?

A. You decide to bag studying and watch your favorite show on T.V. At this point, it's too late to learn the info.

B. Call the class genius and ask her for some pointers, then do some studying.

C. Stay up all night freaking out about the test and praying for a miracle.

That was easy. I wasn't ever afraid to ask for help. In fact, I'd called Carolyn for help with my Spanish homework just last week. Thanks to her, I got a 95 % on my dialogue. It was B for me!

Next question:

2. You're waiting to find out if you got the lead in your school play. The stress is really starting to mess with your head. What do you do?

A. Try to distract yourself by vegging out with your favorite movie.

B. Bite your nails to the nubs — what else is there to do?

C. Go for a run in the park — it always calms you down.

Well, I'd never tried out for a play, but I had run for class president. And waiting to find out if I'd won the election had nearly killed me. I had to admit that I'd watched a lot of bad T.V. that night because I couldn't concentrate on anything else. I clicked on the letter A. Then I read the next question.

3. Math is really hard for you. You're completely lost in class, and you know it's just going to get worse. What's your stress strategy?

A. Ask your folks to get you a tutor once a week to help you over the hump.

B. Stare at your textbook for hours hoping some of the info will sink in.

C. Forget about it. Who needs math when you've got a calculator?

Okay, I knew better than to click C. Math's really important — just ask Josh. He'll give you about a million reasons why. So that left me to choose between A and B. I had to admit that the idea of working with a tutor wasn't my first choice for an afternoon activity. It wasn't nearly as fun as working with a friend. Still, sometimes only a professional would do. I guessed that if I was really lost in math or another subject I would ask for a tutor. So I clicked the letter A.

4. You're already late for softball practice and the field's halfway across town. How do you handle the situation?

A. You're already late, what's a few more minutes gonna do? You may as well stop in the kitchen for a snack — the extra energy will be good for you anyway.

B. Ask your mom or dad to drive you to practice — even though it means you'll have to endure a lecture about lateness along the way. At least you'll get there faster.

C. Hop on your bike and take the shortcut across the highway to practice. It's faster, and you won't have to endure the wrath of your parents.

I had to click the letter B, although I knew why a lot of kids wouldn't. Lectures from your parents are really awful. Like you don't feel bad enough already, right? On the other hand, there would be no sense in making things worse by being even later or getting hurt on a highway.

I waited a moment while the computer tabulated my score.

1. A. 1 point   B. 2 points   C. 3 points
2. A. 1 point   B. 3 points   C. 2 points
3. A. 2 points   B. 3 points   C. 1 point
4. A. 1 point   B. 2 points   C. 3 points

So how do you rate on the stress-o-meter? Read on to find out.

4-6 points: Hello, Cleopatra, queen of denial! Ignoring your stress won't make it go away. Not being prepared for your problems will catch up with you sooner or later. It's best to at least put some effort into dealing with your stress.

7-9 points: You handle stress in the healthiest way possible. While the initial panic gets your heart pumping and your stomach jumping, you use that added adrenaline to accomplish the task at hand. You're on the right track, so keep up the good work!

10-12 points: Uh-oh! When there's stress around, you have a tendency to go right for the panic button. You tend to let your nerves take over completely, and that makes it impossible for you to think clearly. Instead of panicking, try taking some deep breaths and clearing your mind. Then you'll be able to come up with a logical, safe solution to the problem at hand.

Well, that was a relief! I had seven points, which meant I was handling my stress pretty well. Or at least that's what the computer said. I wondered what my score would have been if the computer knew I was just taking the quiz to avoid studying.

"Back to the books," I told my pet mice. They squeaked a reply, which of course I couldn't understand. But my guess was it had nothing to do with history, and everything to do with me giving them another treat. Naturally, I did just that. And while I was at it, I went down to the kitchen for a scoop of mint chocolate chip ice cream. After all, I could eat and study at the same time, couldn't I?

THREE

I STAYED UP pretty late studying and then went to sleep with dates, names, and historical events floating in my head. I actually had a dream that my pets had turned into George Washington and Thomas Jefferson, and blasted off in an Apollo spaceship to become the first presidential mice on the moon. Pretty weird, huh? Still, as I got off the bus at school the next morning, I felt like I had really studied well. I was ready for anything. Well . . . *almost* anything.

"Do you see what I see?" Felicia asked me as we got off the bus in the parking lot.

I didn't have to ask what she was talking about. It was clear she had spotted our friend Sam talking to a tall boy with light brown hair. He was wearing a T-shirt that said *Thunderbirds Swim Team.*

"What's Sam doing talking to Jeffrey?" I wondered out loud.

"Talking? She's not talking," Felicia corrected me. "She's flirting."

Ordinarily, I would say Felicia was exaggerating, which she often did when it came to boy-girl stuff. But not today. Sam *was* flirting with Jeffrey Alderman. Which would have been fine, if Jeffrey was just some ordinary seventh grader. But Jeffrey was a Pop. Or at least the male version of a Pop. And I knew for sure Addie and her friends weren't going to like Sam flirting with him.

I sighed. Sam was still new to the school. And obviously she hadn't figured out all of the unspoken rules yet. But I sure had.

MIDDLE SCHOOL RULE #21:

PROCEED WITH CAUTION WHEN BEGINNING A NEW FRIENDSHIP — ESPECIALLY WHEN THERE ARE POPS INVOLVED. THERE CAN BE SERIOUS PENALTIES FOR TRYING TO BRIDGE THE GAPS BETWEEN GROUPS.

"Let's get her away from him before Addie sees them," Felicia suggested.

But it was too late. Addie had spotted Sam and Jeffrey together. She was halfway across the parking lot and heading straight toward them. She had a tight smile plastered on her lips, but her blue eyes were blazing.

"Jeffrey," I heard Addie say, as she pulled him by the arm. "You just have to hear the new song Dana downloaded. It's totally incredible."

"Uh, yeah, sure," Jeffrey replied. "In a minute, okay? Sam and I were talking about . . ."

"No, it *can't* wait," Addie told him insistently. "The bell's going to ring soon and you won't be able to hear the whole thing."

"But . . ." Jeffrey began.

"Come on," Addie continued. "We're all hanging out over there." The way she said the word *we're* made it clear that Sam was not invited.

Jeffrey looked from Addie to Sam. It was clear from his expression that he was not sure what to do – stay here and talk to someone he obviously liked, or go over to Popworld with Addie.

In the end, the magnetic force that is the Pops pulled him back over to the dark side. "Um . . . I'll talk to you later, 'kay, Sam?" he asked her.

Sam smiled. "Sure. Cheerio, mate."

As soon as Jeffrey and Addie were gone, Felicia and I hurried over to console Sam. The funny thing was, she didn't seem the least bit upset by what had just happened.

"Poor Jeffrey," she said. "I feel bad for him."

"Why?" Felicia asked her. "He was so rude to you. You should be mad."

Sam shook her head. "It's not his fault. He's scared to argue with Addie. She can make life difficult for him if he hangs out with me too much."

"But what about you?" I said. "Aren't you scared Addie could make things hard for you?"

Sam shook her head. "I don't care what Addie thinks about me, so she can't hurt me," she explained. Then she looked over to where Jeffrey and the Pops were standing. Dana and Addie were standing on either side of him.

They looked sort of like guards who were making sure a prisoner didn't escape. "It's too bad Jeffrey is so caught up in being a Pop," Sam continued. "He's nice. And he's really cute."

Felicia looked over to where Jeffrey and the other Pops were standing. "I guess he is," she agreed. "I never noticed before."

"His eyes twinkle just a little bit when he smiles," Sam pointed out.

Felicia nodded. "Josh's do that, too," she said. "I think it's so sweet."

My mind sort of drifted off as Felicia and Sam started talking about cute boys. I had a lot of friends who were boys, but I didn't think of them as boyfriend material or anything. Neither did most of my other friends. In fact, Felicia was the only one of my friends who was into boys that way — until now. I had to admit I was kind of glad Felicia had Sam to talk to about this stuff now. It usually made me a little uncomfortable when she talked about how cute Josh was. I didn't think of him like that. Still, I wished Sam's crush was on someone other than Jeffrey Alderman.

"Hey, have any of you guys seen Liza?" Marilyn asked as she and Carolyn walked over to where Felicia, Sam, and I were talking.

"She wasn't on the bus this morning," Carolyn added.

I took one look at the twins and started to laugh. Marilyn was wearing a blue sweater with a big, glittery M on the front. Carolyn was in a green sweater with a glittery C on it.

"Our mom is making us wear these," Carolyn explained.

"She sewed them on half of our sweaters," Marilyn added. "And we're in huge trouble if we try to switch them."

"We won't. This is embarrassing enough," Carolyn said. "I'm not risking her doing anything worse — like tattooing our names on our foreheads or something."

I giggled at the idea of any mom ever tattooing anything on her kids. "Oh, those aren't so bad," I told the twins, trying to make them feel better. But we all knew the big glitter-covered letters were pretty awful.

"Anyway, I'm wondering what happened to Liza," Carolyn said.

"I hope she didn't oversleep and miss the bus," Marilyn added.

"She wouldn't do that," I assured the twins. "She knows the big history test is first period today."

"Maybe she *wanted* to miss the test," Marilyn suggested.

"Yeah, these things make her a little nervous," Carolyn added.

"More than a little," I murmured in agreement. We all knew that Liza and tests were a bad combination, which was something I didn't completely understand. When you talked to Liza you could tell how smart she was.

So I could never figure out why she always did so poorly on tests.

"I remember Liza during the test last year," Marilyn told us.

"She was really freaked out afterward," Carolyn recalled.

"It's a really hard test," Marilyn explained.

I shivered nervously. *A really hard test.* I figured the twins knew what they were talking about, since they'd taken the test last year.

I didn't want to hear another word about it. Whatever the twins might say would only make me more nervous. I figured it was better for me to just get to class early and get my thoughts together before my first period teacher handed out the papers.

"Hey, Liza," I greeted my pal as I sat down at our lunch table that afternoon. "I didn't think you were coming in today."

"Why not?" Liza asked me.

I didn't know how to answer that. I didn't want to say that maybe she had skipped the test because it would be too hard for her. That would just hurt her feelings. But since I'd already brought it up, I had to say something. "Um . . . Marilyn and Carolyn just mentioned you weren't on the school bus today, so I figured . . ."

"Hey, Liza," my friend Marc said, as he plopped his tray down next to mine. "I thought you were out today," he interrupted me. "The twins said you weren't on the bus."

Liza shook her head. "I wasn't. My dad gave me a ride to school this morning."

"But no one saw you in the halls before the test, either," Marc pressed her. "Josh and I both looked for you on our way to class."

Before Liza could answer him, Sam, Chloe, and Josh arrived at our table with their trays in hand. "Liza, you're here!" Sam exclaimed. "That's funny. The twins said you weren't on the bus."

"Boy, news really flies fast around here. If my not being on the school bus can be considered news," Liza joked. "I was just telling these guys that I got a ride to school with my dad today. That's why I wasn't on the bus."

"Wasn't that test hard this morning?" Chloe asked as she plopped down in her seat. She looked totally wiped out. "How was I supposed to remember what day the U.S. got involved in World War II?"

"I got so confused I practically forgot what year the War of *1812* happened," I joked.

"That's kind of like asking what color an orange is," Chloe said with a giggle.

"Exactly," I said. My friends and I all laughed.

"I didn't think the test was too bad," Josh said when the laughter died down.

"Maybe not for you, braniac," Marc teased him. "But for the rest of us, it was definitely brutal. I mean, who remembers things like the definition of the Stamp Act?"

I looked over at Liza. Once again, she was staring into

space and avoiding our conversation. The test must have really gotten to her. She was too freaked out to even discuss it.

At that moment, Carolyn and Marilyn appeared at the table.

"Liza!" Carolyn exclaimed.

"We thought you weren't coming in today," Marilyn added

"*Her dad drove her to school!*" Josh, Chloe, Sam, Marc, and I all shouted in unison. Then we started laughing again. Not for any real reason. I guess we were just all giddy after that long, hard test. Apparently we were laughing pretty loud, though, because kids at other tables turned around and stared at us.

Speaking of staring, Sam's eyes were focused across the room on the Pops' table.

"Why are you looking at *them*?" Chloe asked her.

"Not them," Sam corrected her. "*Him*. Jeffrey. Isn't he adorable?"

Chloe shrugged. "Never thought about it."

"Well, I have," Sam said. "I think about him a lot."

"Forget it, Sam," Marilyn told her.

"Yeah, he's a Pop," Carolyn added. "They stick together like glue."

"I think Jeffrey's different," Sam insisted.

Chloe sighed. "Look, Sam, you're new here. So maybe you don't completely understand. I know you feel like you and Jeffrey could be like Romeo and Juliet, and nobody likes a good drama more than I do. But you and Jeffrey . . . that's not gonna happen."

"Chloe!" Liza exclaimed. "That's so mean."

"I'm actually trying to be nice," Chloe insisted. "I'm saving Sam from a big disappointment."

"Look, I know what I'm up against," Sam said. "My first few days here, I sat at that table, remember?"

How could we forget? When Sam had first arrived at Joyce Kilmer Middle School, the Pops had claimed her as their own. But then some of the Pops started worshipping Sam more than Addie. And Addie Wilson was not one to be pushed off of her Pop throne. So she'd seen to it that Sam was banished from Popland. Forever.

But the Pops' loss was our gain. Sam was one of the coolest, nicest people I'd ever met. But she was also pretty naïve when it came to the middle school social hierarchy.

Lucky for her, the rest of us weren't. "I have to agree with Chloe on this one," Josh told Sam. "The probability of a Pop and a non-Pop . . ."

"We're not talking about math probabilities here," Liza insisted. "We're talking about people."

"But he's a Pop, and Sam's not," Chloe insisted. "And we all know that could never work."

"Come on. It's not like we're a different species," Sam told her.

"Almost," Chloe replied. "Those kinds of things only work out in the movies."

"Hey, don't underestimate the power of movies," Marc

insisted. "A lot of times life imitates art, you know. Maybe Sam and Jeffrey could get together."

I grinned. Marc's dream in life was to be a big time movie director. So I wasn't surprised to hear him defend the power of film. But I wasn't sure he was right this time. I mean, I would have liked to believe a romance between a Pop and a non-Pop was possible, but I wasn't so sure.

At just that moment, Addie, Sabrina, Claire, and Dana — the girl Pops from their lunch table — filed past us. I watched a smile form on Sam's face as they headed into the bathroom and the door shut behind them.

"I'm going to go over there to talk to Jeffrey!" she said excitedly.

"Are you nuts?" Carolyn asked.

"If they come out and see you at their table, they'll be furious," Marilyn told her.

"Oh, come on you guys," Liza said. "What could they actually do?"

I sighed. About a million mean things came to mind.

But Sam wasn't about to give up this chance to talk to Jeffrey. She stood up and fluffed out her dark hair. "Wish me luck," she said.

"I'll do better than that," Liza said. "I'll go with you."

We all stared at her. Usually, Liza was very, very shy. She got embarrassed really easily. In fact, she was the only kid in school who blushed more often than I did. But here she was, bravely walking over into enemy territory, just to give moral support to a friend.

"Liza, are you out of your mind?" Chloe asked her. "Jeffrey's a Pop. He's gonna be awful to you guys."

"People can change," Liza told her as she walked off.

Some people maybe, but not Addie Wilson. A few minutes later, I saw her step out of the girls' room and begin heading back to her table. She stopped the minute she got a look at Sam and Liza talking to Jeffrey and his friend Aaron.

"Oh, man," I murmured, watching Addie's blue eyes shrink into angry little slits. Her upper lip curled under until it almost disappeared. "This is going to be bad," I murmured.

But not just then it wasn't. At that moment, the bell rang. Like the rest of us mere mortals, Addie had to get to her next class. Which meant that Sam and Liza had literally been saved by the bell!

I WAS NEVER so glad to see a weekend arrive. For starters, I needed a rest after that history test. But even more importantly, I was hoping Addie and her pals would cool down by Monday. Because, while Sam might be able to handle Addie's venom, Liza is different. She's such a nice, gentle person. I was worried about how dealing with the Pops would affect her.

All weekend long I kept thinking about how Liza had gone over to sit at the Pops table with Sam. It was so out of character for her. I know she said people could change, but this was a *total* flip-flop. Usually Liza was the peacemaker, the one who avoided arguments at all cost. But this time she'd joined Sam in what could only be called a declaration of war.

That was no exaggeration, either. The Pops were as territorial as any army, and they were every bit as willing to fight for it. Which was why I wasn't the least bit surprised when Sam called me on Sunday afternoon and told me she'd been getting weird calls at home.

"At first they were just someone calling and hanging up," she told me. "And then it was all these dumb jokes, like 'Is your refrigerator running? Then you'd better catch it.'"

"Oh, come on," I groaned. "That's the oldest, dumbest joke there is. Even Rachel wouldn't tell that one."

"It was no big deal. I knew who it was. It didn't really get annoying until they started blowing a whistle into the receiver," Sam told me.

"Ooh, that had to hurt your ear," I commiserated with her.

"Yeah, but not as badly as Dana's punishment hurt, I'm sure," Sam said with a giggle. "My mother answered the phone one time. Boy was she mad when they blew that whistle in her ear. She checked the caller ID on our landline. The name Harrison popped right up on the screen, so my mom called Dana's and told her what had been happening. Dana wasn't allowed to sleep at Maya's Saturday night. She was grounded."

I gulped. So much for the Pops' calming down over the weekend. They were going to be madder than ever now. "Did they pull any phony phone calls on Liza?" I asked.

"I don't know," Sam admitted. "I didn't get to talk to her. But I wouldn't worry too much, Jen. Liza's tougher than you think."

I sighed. Sam was new to the school. She didn't know Liza nearly as well as I did. Still, I hoped she was right. The past few days had to have been hard enough on Liza as it was.

"Besides, I doubt Dana's gonna be allowed near a phone for a while," Sam told me. "Her mom was soooo mad!"

Sam sounded very triumphant. But I had a feeling

she'd be singing a different tune come Monday. In fact, we all might. For some reason, whenever the Pops got angry with one person in our group of friends, they were mean to all of us.

The thought of that made me nervous. Which made me hungry. For some reason, nerves and hunger pains always seem to go together with me. I decided what I needed was to take my mind off of all this middle school drama by baking some cookies. And I knew just where to look for the recipe — middleschoolsurvival.com!

Once I'd found the snack I was searching for, all I needed were the ingredients, and an adult to help me with the oven. (I'm still not really allowed to bake on my own yet. My parents are soooo overprotective!) "MOM!" I shouted loudly as I raced down the stairs with the print-out of the recipe in my hands. "Wanna make some cookies?"

Nice 'n' Nutty Quick Cookies

You will need:

   1 cup peanut butter
   1 cup sugar
   1 egg
   1 teaspoon baking soda

Here's what you do:

   Preheat oven to 350°. Use a mixer to combine the peanut butter and sugar. Mix until smooth. Then use a wooden spoon to stir in the baking soda and the egg. Roll the dough into balls, and place them approximately 1½ inches apart on a greased cookie sheet. Bake the cookies (at 350 degrees) for 8 minutes or until the edges turn golden brown. Be careful not to over-bake them or they will become hard and crumbly. Remove the cookies from the oven and allow them to cool before eating. Makes 6-10 cookies.

CONGRATULATIONS LIZA MARKS AND JOSH EISEN!

That was the sign that greeted us as the buses pulled into the school parking lot Monday morning.

"What's that all about?" Felicia wondered as we got off the bus.

It didn't take us long to find out. "Did you hear?" Rachel shouted as she ran across the parking lot with Chloe. "Our school has two finalists in the statewide history contest."

"Josh is a finalist?" Felicia squealed excitedly, looking up at the sign. "Ooh! Where is he?"

"Never mind Josh," Chloe said. "Everyone knew he was going to do well. But did you see who is the finalist from the seventh grade? Liza!"

That *was* the real shocker. In fact, I was so surprised I couldn't even speak. I just stood there, staring at the sign.

"You know what's totally cool about this?" Rachel suggested. "The two finalists from this school are *our* friends!"

"We are so awesome!" Chloe agreed.

Just then, Josh's school bus pulled into the parking lot. Marc, who took the same bus as Chloe, was waiting for him. As Josh walked over to us, Marc followed at his side, making sure his video camera remained focused on Josh's face the whole time.

"This is going to be a great scene for the film," Marc said as he filmed Josh. "A genius's triumphant march."

I knew exactly what film Marc was talking about. He was making a documentary about what life in middle school was *really* like. It was kind of like MTV's *The Real World*, but with sixth, seventh, and eighth graders.

"Oh, Josh, I'm so proud of you," Felicia said, racing over and wrapping her arms around his neck.

Josh blushed so red I thought his cheeks might explode. Even though everyone knows he and Felicia are boyfriend and girlfriend, he's still embarrassed about it. And that kind of PDA was too much for him – especially since he knew it had all just been recorded for posterity.

"Uh, thanks," he murmured.

"So when did you find out?" Chloe asked him.

"Last night," Josh told her. "They scored the tests over the weekend. Principal Gold called as soon as she knew."

"Wow! You must have flipped out," Rachel said.

Somehow I couldn't imagine Josh flipping out over anything. He was pretty calm, cool, and collected on a regular basis.

"I knew I had done well," he told Rachel. "So it wasn't a total surprise."

If anyone else had said that, it would have sounded totally conceited. But Josh didn't mean it that way. He was just stating a fact, like any other fact. The Revolutionary War started in 1776. A right triangle has a 90-degree angle. An adjective is a word that describes a noun. He knew he had done well on the test. To Josh they were all the same. Just facts. Actually, there isn't a conceited bone in Josh's body, which is pretty incredible considering he's a genius who also happens to have a black belt in tae kwon do. He's pretty impressive.

"Well, maybe it wasn't a surprise to you, but I bet Liza flipped out," Chloe said. "Has anyone talked to her?"

We all shook our heads. "I haven't seen her yet," I said. "But I can't wait to congratulate her."

"I wonder how she managed it," Chloe said. "That was a tough test."

"Liza's pretty smart," I said, defending our mutual friend.

"Yeah, totally. But Liza and tests are not compatible," Marc said. He looked up at the congratulatory sign that hung above the parking lot. "At least not usually."

"It's definitely big news," Rachel agreed.

"But good news," I reminded her. "*Really* good."

"Congratulations, you guys," an eighth grader named Sonia said as she passed by our lunch table with her tray that afternoon. "Making it to the state finals is huge."

"Seriously. I'm glad somebody from this place could do it," her friend Kristin agreed.

"Thanks," Josh mumbled.

"I still can't believe it's real," Liza admitted.

That was the general consensus. Liza's high score on the exam was a major school-wide surprise.

"Way to go, guys!" Justin Abramowitz, a sixth grader said. He sat down at the table right behind ours with his friend Mitchell. "Totally cool." He turned to me. "Hi, Jenny. Haven't seen you around for a while."

"Yeah. Hey, Justin." I sighed slightly. Justin and I had gone through elementary school together, but ever since we'd been in middle school and traveling in different crowds, he'd never spoken to me. Now he was talking like we were old buddies. Of course, I knew that was only because I was friendly with Liza and Josh, who were pretty much school heroes at the moment. I made a mental note of yet another important middle school rule you'll never see in an orientation handbook.

MIDDLE SCHOOL RULE #22:
YOU'RE ONLY AS COOL AS PEOPLE THINK YOUR FRIENDS ARE.

And right now, everyone thought my friends were cool. So I was kind of cool by association. "Wow! I feel like we're at the celebrity table!" I exclaimed. "Everyone's staring at us."

Marc held his camera up and pointed it at Liza. "Liza Marks, you've just made it to the state finals in the history contest. What are you going to do now?"

"Eat my sandwich," Liza said with a giggle.

"If you can," Sam told her. "This bread is stale."

"Don't break your teeth, Liza," Marilyn told her.

"Yeah, you can't afford to waste valuable studying time at the dentist," Carolyn added.

"You either, Josh," Marilyn said.

"The whole school is depending on you guys," Marc agreed. "You're going to put Joyce Kilmer Middle School on the map!"

"Suppertime . . . yes, it's suppertime . . ." Suddenly, Chloe began singing one of the songs from *You're a Good Man, Charlie Brown* at the top of her lungs as she took a big bite of her sandwich. I guess she got tired of Josh and Liza being the center of attention. Not that she wasn't happy for Liza and Josh. She just couldn't share the limelight for a long time. It wasn't in her DNA.

"How *is* the show coming along, Chloe?" Sam asked, choking back a laugh. I guess she'd figured out what Chloe was doing as well.

"Pretty well," Chloe said. "Of course, I'm not in a lot of scenes, but the ones I am in seem to be in great shape. I've got my solo perfected. I only hope the scenery will be done by the end of this week. The first performance is Friday night."

"It will be," Liza assured her.

"How are you going to get it done when you've got all this history studying to do?" Chloe demanded.

"It's under control," Liza insisted. "You just worry about that solo. Leave the artwork to me."

The play's scenery may have been under control back in the auditorium, but I had a feeling things in the *cafeteria* were about to spin out of control — Jeffrey and Aaron had just stopped at our table.

"Congrats, you guys," Aaron said to Liza and Josh.

"Thanks," Liza said, blushing.

"This is all anyone's talking about," Aaron continued.

Well, not exactly. As I looked across the cafeteria, I could see Addie, Dana, Sabrina, and Claire whispering about something. And from the way they were looking at our table, I was pretty sure it wasn't history.

"Yeah," Jeffrey echoed. He smiled at Sam. "Do you still want me to teach you how to dive at the Community Center pool one afternoon?"

Sam nodded. "I'm really keen to learn. Let me know which day works on your schedule." Because of her English accent, she pronounced that last word, *shedule*, which made it sound so much cooler.

"I've gotta check when I have soccer practice, and then I'll call you," Jeffrey said. He turned his head slightly, which meant the Pops' angry faces were now directly in his line of vision. "Uh . . . we gotta go," he said, tugging slightly at Aaron's sleeve.

Aaron nodded. "Yeah. Well, congrats again, Liza and Josh. You two totally rock."

"Whoa, speaking of rock," Chloe said as they walked away, "I think Aaron and Jeffrey just knocked the foundation of our school hierarchy. Did you see the look on Sabrina's face when they stopped here to talk to us?" She scrunched up her lips into an angry O and crossed her eyes, in a wacky imitation of Sabrina.

I practically fell off my chair laughing. But I stopped giggling a few seconds later as the Pop girls got up and began their daily journey to the girls' room. No sense raising their curiosity about what we'd been talking about.

"Uh-oh. Loo troop coming up on the left," Sam said, trying not to look in the Pops' direction.

I braced myself, certain we were in for an all out confrontation with Addie, Dana, Sabrina, and Claire. Between Sam getting Dana in trouble over the weekend, and Jeffrey and Aaron's quick stopover at our lunch table today, I figured we were about to get some fireworks.

But we didn't. In fact, the Pops didn't even stop at our table on their way to the bathroom. They just kept walking. But as they passed by they murmured the strangest thing. I couldn't even make out what they were saying.

"What was that?" Marilyn asked. "Did they say, 'Cheep, cheep'?"

"Like we were chickens or something?" Carolyn wondered.

"I thought it was 'Cheek, cheek,'" Sam said. "You know, like we were cheeky."

"I don't even know what that means," Josh said.

"It means rude," Sam told him.

"Well, if Josh didn't know what it meant I doubt the Pops do," Chloe told her. "I mean, he's like the smartest kid in school."

Josh shrugged and stared at his food. But he didn't argue with Chloe. How could he? He *was* the smartest kid in school. And surprisingly, we now knew Liza was a close second — at least in history.

"Actually, I thought they were saying 'sweet treat,'" Marc said.

"No, it was 'cheek, cheek,'" Sam insisted.

"'Cheep, cheep,'" Marilyn and Carolyn persisted, sounding a lot like chickens.

"Well, whatever it was, it couldn't have been very important," Liza said.

"Nah. Nothing they ever say is too earth-shattering," Josh agreed.

But my brilliant friend was about to be proven wrong. Big time!

LIZA MARKS CHEATED!

Liza Marks could not possibly have legitimately gotten into the state finals for the history contest. Everyone knows she can't even pass a regular test, never mind one as hard as this one. What, did she suddenly become a genius? We don't think so.

The only thing that has changed is that now Liza is friends with Sam Livingston. Obviously, Sam is a bad influence on Liza. She had to be the one who convinced her to cheat. English people are really sneaky. Remember Benedict Arnold? (You should, he was on the test.) Is it possible Benedict <u>Livingston</u> stole the answers to the test and gave them to Liza? We demand Liza and Sam turn themselves in right now — before our school is even <u>more</u> embarrassed by them!

That was the flier posted in the middle of C wing the next day. I noticed it as I was leaving the school at the end of the day. It was hard to miss — it was printed on hot pink paper.

I had barely finished reading the flier when Chloe popped up behind me.

"Do you believe this?" she asked me without even bothering to say hello.

"Yeah," I replied sadly. "It's so mean. And I bet whoever wrote it taped copies up all over the school." I tore the pink paper I had been reading off the wall and tossed it in a trashcan. That was one less flier for people to read.

"What do you mean *whoever*?" Chloe said. "It's obvious who did it. The Pops. It had to be. Who else is mean enough to do something like this?"

Just then Felicia came over to us. She was carrying a yellow flier with the same message on it. "Isn't this horrible?" she asked. "This is the meanest thing those girls have ever done. And that's saying a lot."

"This is their way of getting even with Liza and Sam for hanging out with Jeffrey and Aaron," I deduced. "I knew they'd do something. But this is extreme, even for them."

"They were also really mad that two kids from our group of friends got into the finals, and no one from theirs did," Felicia reminded me. "So they were doubly angry."

"Oh, come on," Chloe said. "They didn't think any Pops were going to win. Nobody did. Unless this test was about the history of American lip gloss. . . ."

I had to choke back a laugh. That was pretty funny. But

it was far from the truth. The Pops weren't all dumb. For instance, Addie was smart — really smart. She was a whiz at English and French. And apparently she was really good at writing fliers that got people's attention.

"They definitely couldn't say Josh cheated, because everyone knows he's a genius," Felicia said, stating the obvious. "So Liza was an easy choice."

"Exactly," Chloe agreed. "And since Jeffrey likes Sam, they decided to get her in trouble, too."

"They're not going to get into trouble," I insisted. "Not because of some stupid flier. No one's going to take this seriously."

"Unless it's true," Chloe said quietly.

"What?" I asked.

Chloe sighed. "Now you know I love Liza, Jen," she said slowly. "We all do. But didn't it seem the least bit weird to you guys that she finally did well on a test — and it's *this* one?"

"Maybe she's really good at history," Felicia suggested.

"*This* good?" Chloe asked.

"Come on, Chloe," I scolded her. "Liza would never cheat. She's so honest."

"Remember what she said about people changing?" Chloe reminded me. "The old Liza would never go sit with Aaron and Jeffrey."

"And there was that weird thing about her disappearing before the test," Felicia recalled.

"Her dad drove her to school," I reminded her. "Liza told us that herself."

"What was she supposed to say?" Chloe asked. "I was off somewhere studying a cheat sheet?"

Cheat sheet. Suddenly it all fell into place. So that was what the Pops had been saying as they passed by our table at lunch. "You guys are being ridiculous," I told my friends. "Liza and Sam did *not* cheat!"

"Okay, so not Sam," Felicia agreed. "She had no reason to help Liza cheat. It wouldn't benefit her at all. But Liza . . . I mean maybe she was just sick of bombing tests all the time."

I didn't say anything. But I had to admit the idea that Liza could have cheated was nagging at me. There was a lot of evidence against her. And not just that she wasn't on the bus. Marc and Josh hadn't seen her in the hallway before the test, either. She *could* have been off memorizing answers in a bathroom or something.

No! I forced myself to stop thinking that way. Still, Liza's sudden surge of smartness could be considered suspicious. At least to someone who wasn't really her true friend. But was *I* a true friend? Was it possible to be a good friend even if I had my doubts, too? This was all so confusing. I needed someone to tell me the truth. Someone who could look at it all objectively. But no one I knew could do that. They'd all tell me I was a good friend – if only so they didn't hurt my feelings.

But a computer didn't take sides. It only studied the facts. So the minute I got home, I raced over and logged on to middleschoolsurvival.com. A moment later, I had my judge and jury right there on the screen!

What Kind of Friend are You?

Are you the best BFF anyone's ever had? Or do you think the whole friendship thing is overrated? There's only one way to find out if you're true blue or a fair weather friend. You'll have to take this quiz:

1. **There's only one gorgeous blue minidress left in the store and you and your best friend are the same size. You both reach for it at the same time. What do you do?**

    A. Step aside and let your friend have it. She looks better in blue than you do, anyway.
    B. Tell her she looks awful in blue and suggest she try the green one instead.
    C. Make a pact that neither of you will buy the dress, then hit another store together.

Okay, that one wasn't so tough. Clothes weren't a huge deal to me — or to my friends (except Sam, and her style was too unique for any of us to copy). My answer was definitely C.

2. **Your best friend doesn't have the money to join you and your other friends at the movies. You have the money for the**

movie, but could use a little more for popcorn. Your neighbor calls and asks if you know anyone who can feed and walk her dog after school for some extra cash. What do you do?

A. Let your friend earn the money — she needs it more than you do.

B. Keep your mouth shut and earn the extra cash yourself.

C. Offer to split the job with your BFF so you can both go to the movies and share a popcorn.

I knew the real super-duper friend would answer letter A. But I also knew deep down that I'm not that selfless. Besides, I really like movie theater popcorn. I would be more likely to try C, which is what I clicked.

3. Usually . . .

A. Your friends come to you when they have a problem because they know you'll listen to them and keep the conversation to yourself.

B. Your friends like to goof around with you, but they keep the really deep, meaningful conversations for someone else. They know you can't keep anything secret.

C. You can be trusted with the really big secrets. You only let the silly little things slip out — and who cares about them?

Definitely A. I never tell secrets — or I try not to anyway. And my friends come to me for advice a lot. Me, or Liza, anyway.

Liza. I frowned slightly as I remembered why I was taking this quiz in the first place. I really did want to be a good friend to her. Quickly, I read the next question.

4. How would you describe your group of friends?

A. A tight group of pals who share everything and help one another whenever you can.

B. A constantly changing group; you're never really sure who your best friends will be from week to week.

C. A big group of kids that is made up of several different interlocking groups. You all get along, but there are definitely pairs of BFFs in the mix.

A again. Totally. There were no best friends in our group. We're all for one and one for all.

Suddenly, I stopped mid-thought. That's how we had been up until a few weeks ago. But this whole new Sam and Liza alliance was kind of weird. They were hanging out together a lot. Was it possible that they were BFF now? Did they have private secrets they wouldn't share with any of us? Were they doing things together and not inviting the rest of us?

It wasn't exactly a thought I enjoyed considering, but it seemed to be the truth. And there was no point taking the test if I wasn't going to be honest, with the website and with myself. I sighed as I changed my answer to the letter C.

That was the last question. I waited as the computer took a moment to tally up my final score.

You have: One A and Three C's
Okay, it's time to find out where you fall on the good friend scale. Drum roll please!

Mostly A's: Wow. Anyone would be lucky to count you as one of their close friends. You are selfless and caring. Most importantly, you can be trusted to come through when the chips are down.

Mostly B's: *Friend: somebody who has a close personal relationship of mutual affection and trust with another.* That's the dictionary definition of what a friend really is. And that's what you should be striving for. Right now your loyalty is mostly to yourself. Take a good hard look in the mirror, and make the decision to start thinking more about your pals right now!

Mostly C's: This is where most people seem to land on the friendship scale. Basically, you're a good friend — fun to be around and willing to compromise. You also look out for yourself, which is not always a bad thing. Being your own friend is important, too.

I looked at the answers and sighed. Okay, so I wasn't the worst friend in the world. But I wasn't one of the best, either. I was somewhere in the middle.

But I really wanted to be in that A category — trusted

to come through when the chips were down. And boy were the chips down right now as far as Liza was concerned.

I decided right then and there that I believed Liza was innocent, because she was my friend and I trusted her. From that moment on, I was going to make it my business to make everyone else believe in her, too.

Chapter
SIX

BUT CONVINCING EVERYONE else Liza was innocent wasn't going to be easy. The minute my bus pulled into the school parking lot the next morning, I could tell that everyone believed Liza had really cheated. For starters, while the big *Congratulations* banner was still hanging, someone had taken a black marker and crossed Liza's name off. They'd also taken a red marker and written *Cheater* over her name. Whoever was behind this (and I was pretty sure it was the Pops) wanted to get their message across, just in case anyone hadn't seen their fliers.

"Man, this is bad," Felicia said as we stood there together, staring at the banner. "Liza is all anyone can talk about. Rachel and I were on the phone for an hour last night and she didn't even crack one joke."

"Yeah, well, there's nothing funny about this," I agreed.

Just then, Marilyn, Carolyn, and Chloe walked over to us. They were staring at the banner, too.

"I just can't believe it." Marilyn sighed.

"Me, either," Carolyn agreed.

"That makes three of us," Chloe said, shaking her head. "And that's a first!"

I nodded in agreement. It was hard for me to believe anyone could be so mean to Liza.

But apparently, that's not what my friends meant.

"I just don't understand why Liza would cheat," Chloe continued.

"Who says she *did* cheat?" I exclaimed angrily. "Some jerks who aren't even brave enough to sign their fliers? Why would you believe them over our friend?"

"Calm down, Jenny," Marilyn said. "We all love Liza, too."

"We just want to help her," Carolyn added.

"Then start by believing her," I said. "Remember, in this country we're all innocent until we're proven guilty."

"Huh?" Marilyn asked.

"Where did you get that from?" Carolyn wondered.

"The Constitution," I said.

"I guess I got that one wrong on the test," Marilyn replied sheepishly.

"I think I said it was on the base of the Statue of Liberty," Carolyn said.

"Uh, can we get back to Liza?" I interrupted. "This is really important."

"You're right, Jen," Chloe agreed. "Liza is our friend. We should talk to her and find out what really happened. We shouldn't take someone else's word over hers."

I nodded. "Exactly. That's what a real friend would do. And that's what we are. Mostly As on the friendship scale."

Chloe, Felicia, and the twins all stared at me. They had no idea what I was talking about. But before I could explain about the computer quiz I had taken the night before, Sam came running over to us. Tears were flowing down her face. I'd never seen her look so upset. "I HATE Jeffrey! I HATE him!" she exclaimed.

"What happened?" Chloe asked.

"He's such a git!" Sam exclaimed.

"A what?" I asked her.

"It means jerk," Sam translated. "Which is exactly what Jeffrey is. He told me he didn't want to help me learn to dive. He didn't want to talk to me," Sam said between sobs. "He doesn't want to be associated with someone who would help Liza cheat."

"Oh," Felicia said. "That's awful."

I sighed heavily. Poor Sam. She'd been so certain that Addie couldn't find a way to hurt her. But of course, she'd been wrong. It was always a mistake to underestimate Addie and the rest of the Pops.

"Jeffrey thinks I stole the answers from the teachers' lounge and gave them to Liza." Sam gasped for a minute, trying to catch her breath between furious sobs. "Give me a break. I'm new here. I don't even know where the teacher's lounge is. Half the time I can't even find a loo when I need one! Just last week a bunch of eighth graders sent me on a wild goose chase looking for the school swimming pool."

"We don't have one of those," Chloe said gently.

"I found that out — the hard way," Sam replied.

I knew what she meant. Apparently, every year the eighth graders pulled the same swimming pool trick on unsuspecting sixth graders. They'd gotten me on the first day of school.

"Ha!" Just then Addie's voice rang out behind me. I don't know where she came from, but there she was, all smug and cold, with Dana at her side. "So Sam says she didn't steal the answers. You can believe her if you want to. But Liza still cheated. Everyone knows it. Everyone *believes* it. Just look around."

I did. And sure enough, everyone in the school parking lot was staring at the banner. There was a lot of whispering and nodding going on. And if you listened really closely, every now and then someone would say something like, "I knew it!" or "Man, she's in so much trouble."

"Not everyone, Addie," I told her. "*We* don't believe it."

Addie stared at us for a minute and shrugged. "Suit yourselves." She looked around. "Or better yet, why don't you just ask her if it's true or not?"

"We haven't seen her yet," Marilyn said.

"Yeah. She wasn't on the bus," Carolyn added.

"She's probably in Ms. Gold's office with her parents," Dana said. "I bet she's in big trouble for what she's done."

I sighed. I sure hoped Dana was wrong. Because so far the only thing Liza had done for sure was sit down for a few minutes with Aaron and Jeffrey during lunch. And she was certainly being punished for that. I could only hope Ms. Gold wasn't as gullible as the kids in the parking lot.

Dana giggled. "Nice eye makeup, Sam," she said. "Are zebra stripes the big thing in England?"

"What?" Sam wondered. As Dana and Addie walked away, Sam looked at her reflection in a school bus window. All her crying had caused her black mascara to stream down her cheeks in wriggly stripes.

"I . . . um . . . I've gotta go wash up," Sam said, running toward the school building.

"You know, I think *Addie's right*," Chloe told us as Sam left.

Felicia, the twins, and I all stared at her with surprise. "Those are two words I never thought I'd hear you say in one sentence," Felicia said

"I mean, we should just ask Liza if she cheated," Chloe said.

"That's a terrible idea," I countered.

Felicia looked at me. "Why?"

"Because then *she'll* think *we* think she could have cheated," I said.

"Well, don't we?" Felicia asked, her voice all soft, quiet, and scared. "At least a little bit?"

"No!" I exclaimed. I only hoped I sounded more certain than I felt.

About ten minutes later, I was feeling even less certain than before. I had stopped in the bathroom near Ms. Gold's office on my way to my first period English class. I overheard the principal talking to her assistant, Ms. Donoghue. Now I know eavesdropping is bad, but I couldn't help it. First of all, the office door was wide open. And second of all, they were talking about my friend, which sort of made it my business, didn't it?

"Have you contacted Mr. Collins and asked him to take down that banner in the parking lot?" Ms. Gold asked.

"Yes, he's doing it now," Ms. Donoghue replied.

"We can't have vandalized property hanging outside the school," Ms. Gold added. "Oh, and speaking of that sign, Liza Marks won't be in class this morning."

"I'll let her teachers know," Ms. Donoghue replied.

I gulped. Was that some sort of punishment? Had Liza been given a half-day suspension or something?

"How's she holding up, anyway?" I overheard Ms. Donoghue ask the principal.

"About as well as can be expected. This is hard on her," Ms. Gold said. "I was just telling her mother this morning that I thought it was going to be tough on Liza to admit the problem and deal with it," Ms. Gold continued. "But she's doing it."

That stopped me in my tracks. Ms. Gold had spoken to Liza's mother that morning. Which meant Addie and Dana had been right. There had definitely been a meeting with the principal that morning!

"I don't think she's told any of her friends the truth yet," Ms. Gold told Ms. Donoghue.

The truth! Oh man. That sounded bad — as if Liza had been lying to us all this time. Was it possible? Could she have cheated?

"I wonder how they'll take it," Ms. Donoghue replied.

I sighed heavily. So did I.

The bell rang just as I slipped into my seat in English class. Good thing, because Ms. Jaffe, my English teacher, is really tough on us about being late. She takes points off, or makes us write an apology letter, or (and this is the worst) she makes you get up in front of the whole class and apologize for holding things up.

I slid into my seat beside Chloe, and opened up my grammar textbook. We were working on commas, which was something I should have been paying attention to. I'm lousy with commas. I just sort of shove them in the sentence wherever. I once heard someone say that if you were reading the sentence out loud and you paused, that's where the comma should go. So that's pretty much what I do. But apparently, according to English teachers, it's a lot more complicated than that.

I glanced over toward the window where, as usual, Dana and Addie were sitting. I could feel my face tighten just looking at them. Why did they have to embarrass a really nice girl like Liza like that? Then I looked over at Sam, whose face was still slightly streaked with a few remnants of dripped mascara. I wondered why they would drag an innocent person into the mix.

I sighed heavily. I knew the answer to that one. Because they were Pops. And that's what Pops do.

But I wasn't a Pop. I wasn't out to hurt Liza — or anyone for that matter. I was going to help her through this. But it was going to take all of my friends to do that. We had to make sure she knew we didn't care if she cheated, or that she had been suspended for half a day, or anything. Since Chloe was sitting right next to me, I decided to start with her. Quickly, I scribbled something on a piece of paper.

Chloe,
I've got to talk to you after class. It's about Liza, and it's important.

Then I folded the note up really small, waited until Ms. Jaffe was looking the other way, and tossed it onto Chloe's desk.

"Jenny McAfee!" Ms. Jaffe's voice rang out across the classroom. "I certainly hope you placed commas in the correct places in that note you just passed."

I gulped and suddenly remembered another middle school rule no one ever tells you at orientation.

MIDDLE SCHOOL RULE #23:

EVEN WHEN THEY'RE NOT LOOKING RIGHT AT YOU, TEACHERS CAN STILL SEE YOU — ESPECIALLY IF YOU'RE BREAKING THEIR RULES.

"Since you seem so enthusiastic about writing today, I'm going to do something nice for you, Jenny," Ms. Jaffe continued.

I bit my lip. Somehow I didn't think my teacher and I were going to agree on the definition of "something nice."

"I'd like you to write a paragraph about the importance of paying attention during grammar lessons," Ms. Jaffe said. "Be sure to place all of your commas, periods, and semicolons in the right places."

Just as I suspected. This was not going to be fun. And what were semicolons, anyway? I sunk deep down into my chair as I felt the blood rushing to my cheeks. I blushed even harder when I heard Addie and Dana giggling at my bad luck.

Grrr. I really couldn't stand them. Somehow I felt this was sort of their fault. If they hadn't made life so hard for one of my friends, I wouldn't have had to write the note to Chloe and . . .

No. This was one mistake I couldn't blame them for, and I knew it. I was just going to have to suck it up and write the paragraph. It wasn't a big deal. At least not compared to what Liza was up against.

"Boy, that was tough luck today," Chloe said to me in the hallway after class. "I can't believe you got caught."

I frowned. "Yeah, it stinks," I agreed. "But there are worse things." I paused for a minute as Addie and Dana walked by. They looked at me and started laughing.

"Like them," Chloe said.

I nodded and glanced up at the hall clock. I only had a few minutes to get to my next class. I definitely did not want to get in trouble again, so there wasn't time to tell her about Liza right now. "I'll talk to you at lunch," I said, turning to leave.

"I'm going to be late for lunch," she said. "I have to sell tickets for *You're A Good Man, Charlie Brown.*"

"Oh. Well, that sounds like fun."

Chloe shrugged. "I'm selling them with Cassidy," she explained. "That kind of takes the fun out of it."

"She's nice, Chloe," I said. "Everyone else likes her."

"She didn't steal the lead role away from everyone else," Chloe explained.

"She didn't *steal* the part of Lucy from you," I told Chloe. "She just got it. She's an eighth grader. They probably figured you have plenty of time to get the lead in a school play. Cassidy's graduating this year. This was her last chance."

Chloe nodded. "That's what my mom said, too." She paused. "Anyway, what did you want to talk to me about?"

I frowned as I saw the seconds ticking away. "No time now," I said as I ran off. "I'll have to tell you later."

Chapter
SEVEN

BY THE TIME I got to lunch, mostly everyone was there — Sam, the twins, Marc, and Josh. Everyone but Chloe and Liza. It seemed to be the perfect time to tell them about what I'd overheard.

"Okay, so Liza is in trouble," I told my friends. "Principal Gold talked to her parents today. And I think she had a half-day suspension. That's probably why she's not here right now."

"A half-day suspension," Marilyn repeated. "Wow."

"That's worse than what we got for cheating on the math test," Carolyn added.

"Well, this was a way more important test, I guess," I said. "The thing is, we have to be really supportive of her now. Everyone's going to be mad at her for embarrassing our school in the contest, but we can't be."

"I'm so bummed," Josh said. "I really hoped we could go to the finals together."

"It just doesn't make sense," Marc said. "Liza's not like that. She's totally honest. She's . . . *here!*"

Marc stopped mid-sentence and pointed at the cafeteria door. There stood Liza, with a brown paper bag in hand. She smiled as she spotted us all at the table.

"Now just act naturally," I said, keeping my teeth clenched behind a big smile. "Don't let on we were talking about her."

"Hey, guys, sorry I'm late," Liza said as she sat down next to Marc. "I had some . . . um . . . some stuff to do this morning."

"We know," Sam said. Then she noticed us all glaring at her. "I mean, it's been a crazy morning." She turned her head toward the Pops' table, looked at Jeffrey and sighed.

For a minute there was complete silence at the table. No one was quite sure what to say next. It was getting very uncomfortable. There was nothing normal about the way we were acting.

And then Chloe arrived. She came racing over to the table with a look of absolute panic on her face. Totally normal . . . for Chloe anyway. "You guys, I'm doomed!" she exclaimed frantically.

"Whoa, calm down," Sam said. "Take a breath."

"It can't be that bad," I added.

"Oh, yes it can," Chloe insisted. "It's worse than bad. It's the most horrendous thing ever."

"What happened?" Marc asked, pulling out his video camera, so he could be sure to catch the catastrophe on video.

"Cassidy sprained her ankle — really bad," Chloe said, sadly plopping down into an empty seat.

I looked at Chloe oddly. Somehow that didn't sound

particularly horrendous to me. A little painful maybe, but to Cassidy, not Chloe.

"How'd she do that?" Josh asked.

"She was dancing on the table outside the auditorium, trying to attract people to buy show tickets," Chloe explained. "She fell off the table."

"The show," Sam repeated. "I almost forgot about that. You're her understudy, right?"

Chloe nodded.

"So this is a good thing — for *you* anyway," Sam continued.

"No. It's terrible," Chloe said.

We all stared at her in surprise. Chloe had been dying to play Lucy in the school play. And now she had the chance. Why was she all upset about it?

"I never learned the lines," Chloe said. "And now everyone expects me to know them. The dress rehearsal is Friday — three days from now! And the first show's Saturday. How am I supposed to learn a whole show's worth of lines by then?"

"Oh," Marilyn said quietly.

"That *is* bad," Carolyn agreed.

"Not necessarily," Sam said. "Maybe you don't have to learn the lines, Chloe."

"What? Am I supposed to just ad lib an entire show?" Chloe asked incredulously.

Sam shook her head. "Of course not. But you could use

those things they use on TV, you know, the cards with the words on them. What do you call them?"

"Cue cards?" Chloe asked.

Sam nodded.

"That won't work," Chloe told her. "Cue cards only work on TV because they're behind the camera and no one can see the actors using them. In a theater, everyone would see. The cue card person would be blocking the first row."

Sam nodded slowly and bit her lip. I could tell she was thinking about something. "What if we cut up a script and glued the pages all over the stage?"

"You mean like on the piano, or the side of the dog house, or even on my baseball glove?" Chloe mused, suddenly getting the idea.

Sam nodded. "Anywhere you have to stand while you're saying your lines. Then only you would be able to see that you were actually reading the lines. The audience would never know."

"Cheat sheets," Chloe said as the idea formed in her head.

"CHLOE!" Josh, Marc, Marilyn, Carolyn, and I all shouted at once.

"What?" Chloe asked.

I shifted my eyes slightly in Liza's direction, hoping she wouldn't notice. But she did, of course.

"What?" Liza asked me. She stopped and studied all of

our faces. "Wow, you guys think I cheated on that test," she said slowly, as the realization hit her.

"No, we, um . . . of course not," I said. I didn't think I sounded very convincing.

Neither did Liza. "I was sure you guys would know me better than that," she said, looking as though she was going to cry. "I don't care what the Pops think. But you're all supposed to be my friends."

"We *are*, Liza," Marilyn told her.

"No matter what," Carolyn agreed.

"We don't care that you were on a half-day suspension today, Liza. Honest," Marc assured her.

"A what?" Liza sounded surprised.

"It's okay, Liza. We know and we don't care," I told her.

"I don't know what you're talking about," Liza said. "I wasn't suspended today. I was at the doctor's office."

Oops. Guess I'd gotten that one wrong. "But I heard Ms. Gold say she'd talked to your mother and . . ."

"Ms. Gold and my mother have been talking a lot. Ever since I found out . . ." Liza stopped mid-sentence and took a deep breath. "I wasn't going to tell anyone," she said slowly. "But I sort of had to have these tests taken."

"Oh, no!" Chloe exclaimed dramatically. "Are you okay? Do you need an operation or . . ."

Liza shook her head. "Not those kind of tests. These are like written tests, computer tests, oral tests, and stuff like that."

"Why would you take extra tests?" Sam asked her.

"They're the kind of tests they give you when they're trying to figure out what your problem is with school-work," Liza explained. "And it's no secret that I have trouble with some tests and stuff."

No one knew what to say to that. Of course we all knew. We just didn't want her to *know* we knew.

"Well, it turns out that I have a learning disability," Liza said. "I don't always understand things the way other people do. I have to do things a little differently in order to do well in school. I've been working with a special tutor since the summer."

"But you did so well on the test," Josh said. "How could you if . . ."

Liza smiled. "I'm really good in history," she told him. "I love it. I read history books just for fun."

"But you didn't do so well in history last year," Marc reminded her.

"I know," Liza agreed. "That's because while I'm good in history, I'm lousy with history tests. Especially those ones where you have to use a number two pencil to fill in the dots."

"So how did you do so well on this test?" I asked her. "We had to fill in the dots on the answer sheet."

"I actually didn't have to do that," Liza explained. "Since I have a learning disability, the school changes things a little bit for me. I circled the answers right in the booklet, instead of using the answer sheet. And I get extra time when I take tests because it takes me longer to read and understand the questions. So I came in early on the morning of the history test. I had to take it in Ms. Gold's office."

"Oh," I said quietly. Now I understood why Liza hadn't been on the bus that morning, and why no one had seen her in the halls before school started.

"It turns out that I'm pretty smart, actually," Liza said proudly. "I just have these problems. But I'm working with my tutor to overcome them. That's where I was this morning — there was a meeting between my tutor, the doctor who gave me the tests, my mom, and me."

"So your mom wasn't in school today meeting with Principal Gold?" I asked her.

Liza looked at me curiously. "Where would you get that idea?" she wondered.

I sighed. So much for eavesdropping. "Never mind," I murmured. "I'm just so sorry we ever doubted you."

Liza smiled at me. "It's okay. It did seem suspicious, I guess. And I should have probably told you guys about all this ages ago. I guess I just wanted to keep it to myself for a while. Actually, it's a good thing that we figured it all out. I don't feel so stupid anymore. I actually feel kind of smart."

There was definitely a new confidence in her voice. Which could explain why she'd suddenly gotten so gutsy — like being brave enough to go over to the Pops' table the other day. People *could* change. She was right about that.

Unfortunately, the Pops hadn't changed. Their mean

retaliation for Liza and Sam's move had been perfectly predictable.

"We should have known better than to believe those fliers," Sam apologized to Liza. "Especially since they were posted by people who were too chicken to sign their names to them."

"Even though we all know who did it," I added, staring across the cafeteria at the Pops' table.

"Anyway, I'm glad I don't have to go to that state finals history bee all by myself," Josh said. "You can still do that, right, Liza?"

Liza nodded. "That's all done out loud. I don't need any extra reading time or anything. I'll be standing right there with all of the other finalists."

I grinned. She sounded so proud when she said that. And she had a right to. It was a huge deal to be a state finalist.

"Okay, I'm sorry to break this up, but can we get back to my problem now?" Chloe asked. "I'm the one in the middle of a major trauma!"

"A drama trauma." Marilyn laughed.

"Would Chloe have any other kind?" Carolyn wondered.

Chloe laughed despite herself. She knew she was a total drama queen. Only this time, she had a right to be.

"I think that cheat sheet thing could work," Chloe thought out loud. She turned to Liza. "Can you help me put them in places where the audience won't see them?"

Liza frowned. "Chloe, this is a mistake. You're better off just staying up really late the next few nights and learning . . ."

"I can't learn the lines that fast," she insisted. "You've got to help me."

"Okay," Liza agreed finally. "But I feel like something bad's gonna happen. Cheaters always get caught. Just ask them," she added, jokingly pointing at Marilyn and Carolyn. The twins looked down at the big, glittery M and C monograms on their shirts and sighed.

But Chloe would not change her mind. "This will work," she assured Liza. "There's nothing to worry about."

Chapter
EIGHT

THAT AFTERNOON, Liza let me come into the auditorium with her as she put the finishing touches on the set for the show.

"I don't think this whole cheat sheet thing is going to work," she said as she taped a cue card with Chloe's lines on it to the side of Snoopy's doghouse. "But I promised I would help her."

"You know Chloe," I replied. "Once she's decided on something, there's no changing her mind about it." I looked around the auditorium. Some of the actors in the play were going over scenes in other parts of the auditorium while Liza worked on the stage. "Where is Chloe, anyway?" I asked.

"At a costume fitting," Liza told me. "She isn't as tall as Cassidy, so things had to be hemmed." She crawled into the doghouse to check on the inside of the roof.

I was so busy watching Liza that I didn't notice Addie and Dana entering the auditorium. Considering that neither of them had anything to do with the play, I knew they could only be there for one reason — to be mean to Liza.

"Oh, look! There's Liza Marks in the doghouse," Addie

said as she came near the stage. "Isn't that where people go when they're in big trouble?"

"Liza's not in any trouble, because she didn't cheat," I told Addie. "She made it to the history finals fair and square."

"I find that really hard to believe," Dana said.

"What *I* find hard to believe is why you and your friends are so angry and jealous all the time," I said. Then I gasped slightly. I couldn't believe I'd had the guts to say that to two of the most popular girls in our school.

Neither could Addie. "Us, jealous of *you guys*?" Addie said with a laugh. "Be real, Jenny."

"You *are* jealous, Addie. You're jealous that people are making a fuss over someone besides you. But Josh and Liza did something really amazing. They deserve it. And you were jealous that Jeffrey liked Sam, too." I was really nervous while I was talking. I knew Addie could freak out at any minute and say something really awful back to me. But I was tired of her and her friends being so mean to other people. So I kept on talking. Because if I took even the slightest breath, or paused just for a second, I might not have the guts to keep on going.

"You don't have to be someone's best friend to be happy for them," I continued telling Addie and Dana. "Like I was happy for you, Addie, when the dance you planned was a big success."

Addie and Dana just stared at me. They weren't quite

sure what to say. I think they were in shock that I'd managed to stand up to them. I know *I* was. I stood there, and waited for them to scream at me, or threaten me. But they didn't. Instead, they just turned and started to walk away.

Of course, that didn't last very long. Pops might stumble, but they never get thrown completely. After a few steps, Dana spun around and glared at me. "Liza may have won something, but you can bet Chloe is going to be a loser. And we're going to be sitting in the front row on Saturday night to watch her make a fool out of herself."

I sighed as I watched Liza glue a cue card to the inside of the baseball glove Chloe would be wearing in the baseball game scene of the show. I sure hoped Chloe would be able to get through the show without messing up. If she didn't, the Pops were going to come down really hard on her. There was nothing they liked better than having someone to make fun of.

"No one is supposed to be watching the dress rehearsal, so you guys are going to have to be really quiet back here," Chloe whispered to Sam and me as she ushered us to a little backstage area. "If anyone asks, you're helping Liza with the props."

"We *are* helping Liza with the props," I reminded her. "She asked us to, remember?"

Chloe nodded nervously. "Oh, yeah, right. Good. So that works out perfectly."

"Don't be so stressed, mate," Sam urged. "It'll be fine. The lines are written down for you. You can't possibly muck it up."

"I know," Chloe said, sounding like she was trying to convince herself. "It's just a little pre-show jitters."

"It's not a show, just a dress rehearsal," Sam reminded her.

"True," Chloe said. "No pressure."

But there was a ton of pressure, and we all knew it. This was the first time Chloe was ever running through the entire play in the part of Lucy. And it was the only rehearsal she was going to have before the real performance tomorrow night.

"Okay, gang, let's put on a show," Mrs. Dahms, the theater teacher said, clapping her hands. "Remember, no matter what happens, keep on going. I don't want any stopping. Be professional. Pretend there's a real audience out there."

Mr. Sabatino, our school music teacher, began playing the overture on the piano. Then the actors came on stage. I found myself getting really into the show. The kids who were playing Charlie Brown and his friends were doing a great job. Almost professional. Even Chloe seemed to know what she was doing. She walked around the stage, saying her lines. And if the other cast members knew she was reading from the cards that had been glued to the piano, the doghouse, and the other scenery, they didn't let on. Maybe they hadn't noticed after all.

Bam! Okay, so much for not noticing. It was hard to miss Chloe walking right into the side of the doghouse as she tried to read a cue card Liza had taped there for her.

"Oops. Sorry," Chloe apologized. "I . . . uh . . . I had trouble making out one of the . . . "

"Don't apologize, Chloe," Mrs. Dahms said. "Just keep going."

"Yeah. Right," Chloe said. She took a deep breath and became Lucy again. "Anyway . . . Charlie Brown, you . . ."

"Chloe, it's my line," Jorge Mendez hissed.

"But it says . . ." Chloe began. Then she stopped. She was supposed to be Lucy right now. She couldn't argue with Jorge. She had to keep quiet, and let him say his line first. Knowing Chloe, that couldn't have been easy.

"Okay, this is not so good," Sam whispered to me.

"It's not so bad, either," Liza pointed out, trying to remain hopeful. "Chloe's not the only one to mess up tonight."

That was true. Actually, she wasn't doing too badly. I watched as Chloe and Andrew Mason, the boy who was playing Schroeder, went over to the big toy piano Liza had constructed.

Chloe lay her head down on top of the piano. Liza had glued a cue card there, but when Chloe tried to read the card, she was too close up to be able to see the words clearly. She sat up slightly, and leaned on her elbow to get a better view. "Schroeder, do you think . . ."

Wham! Just then, Chloe's elbow went right through the cardboard top of the piano. One of the wooden legs collapsed.

"I'm sorry," Chloe apologized to Liza, Mrs. Dahms, and Andrew. "I couldn't see the words, and when I shifted my elbow I . . ."

"You couldn't see the *what*?" Mrs. Dahms's voice scaled up nervously as she repeated Chloe's sentence. Obviously, the teacher had forgotten all about not stopping the rehearsal for anything.

"The words," Chloe repeated nervously.

"She has cheat sheets glued all over the stage," Andrew told Mrs. Dahms.

"I just wanted to make sure I remembered all of my lines," Chloe said. "I mean I only just got this part."

"You've been the understudy for the part of Lucy since rehearsals began," Mrs. Dahms reminded her.

"But I never thought Cassidy would hurt herself," Chloe insisted.

"An understudy has to be ready for the unexpected," Mrs. Dahms reminded her. "It's part of the job."

Chloe frowned. She knew that. She just hadn't taken it very seriously.

"Now, what are we supposed to do? The show is tomorrow night," Mrs. Dahms said. "You're letting everyone in the cast down, Chloe. Not to mention all of the people who have purchased tickets to the performance."

Chloe started to cry. She knew she'd messed up big time. She didn't have to be reminded of it by Mrs. Dahms.

I couldn't stand watching her feel so badly. "She'll be ready," I piped up suddenly. Then I gasped, surprised by the sound of my own voice. It wasn't like me to just butt in like that. But butt in is exactly what I'd done.

"Who are *you?*" Mrs. Dahms asked me.

"Jenny McAfee," I said. "I'm helping Liza with the props tonight, and at the show."

"Oh," Mrs. Dahms said. "And how do you propose Chloe will learn all these lines by tomorrow?"

"I'm going to help her. All of her friends are. We'll stay up all night if we have to," I assured the drama teacher. "Chloe already knows all the songs, don't you, Chloe?"

Chloe stared at me, her mouth wide open. She had never seen me like this before. Neither had I, come to think of it. But our group of friends had never had an emergency quite like this before, either. Somehow, Chloe managed to nod in Mrs. Dahms's direction.

"And she's learned a lot of Cassidy's lines just by hearing them over and over at rehearsals," I continued. "Right, Chloe?"

Chloe nodded again.

"The cheat sheets were just there to make sure she got everything right," I continued. "But now *we'll* make sure of it instead. We're going to have a sleepover and spend the whole night making sure Chloe learns everything."

Mrs. Dahms considered that for a moment. "Okay. We'll have a special run-through tomorrow morning," she said finally. "We may as well call it quits tonight — that will give Chloe extra time to learn her lines." The drama teacher turned to me. "I certainly hope your plan works, Jenny."

I sighed heavily. So did I.

Chapter
NINE

"OKAY, CHLOE. NOW LET'S DO THIS SCENE AGAIN." Rachel said later that night as my friends and I sat in the middle of my bedroom floor rehearsing with Chloe. "Remember, I'm your little brother and I'm carrying my security blanket . . ."

"I can't take it anymore," Felicia groaned. "We've been through this a dozen times."

"And we'll go through it a dozen more, until Chloe knows every word," I told her, sounding more like a strict teacher than a kid. "This is *important*, Felicia."

"I know. But I'm exhausted," Felicia said. She paused for a minute, realizing what she'd just said. "I can't believe it. This is a sleepover, and I actually feel like sleeping."

"I know," Marilyn said.

Carolyn seconded that with a loud yawn.

"The sleepovers back home weren't like this," Sam mentioned to me.

"Ours aren't usually, either," I told her. "This is a special situation."

"Back home we play games," Sam continued, "eat junk food and talk about . . ."

"Boys!" Felicia giggled. "We do that here, too."

"You are *so* boy crazy," Liza teased Felicia.

"I am not," Felicia insisted.

We all giggled at that. "Yes you are, and I can prove it!" I exclaimed as I leaped up, went over to my computer, and logged onto middleschoolsurvival.com. "I saw this quiz the other day . . . oh yeah, here it is. It's called 'Are You Boy Crazy?'"

"It's time for a five-minute break, anyway," Marilyn said.

"A boy-crazy test is perfect for you, Felicia," Rachel said.

"Let's see what the quiz says before we jump to any conclusions," Felicia told her.

"Felicia's right," I said. "Maybe she's not boy crazy after all."

Everyone laughed. We all knew that was definitely not the truth. I started to read the quiz out loud.

Are You Boy Crazy?

Boys! You can't live with them and you can't live without them. Either way, they can make you totally crazy, but only if you let them. Are you totally obsessed with the males of our species? There's only one way to determine whether or not you're totally boy crazy. You've got to take the test.

1. How many times a day do you think about boys?

    A. Once a day

    B. Between five and seven times a day

    C. All day long

"Well," Felicia said slowly. "I guess I think about them all day long. But it's not my fault. There are a lot of boys in our school. They're always around. It's hard *not* to think about them."

"True," Rachel agreed. "But what's your excuse for dreaming about them all night?"

Felicia blushed. "How do you know what I dream about?" she asked.

"Your red cheeks are a real giveaway, mate," Sam said.

We all laughed, and I clicked on the letter C.

"Okay, next question," I said.

2. What's your reaction when you spot a cute new guy in front of you in the cafeteria line?

    A. Your heart starts to pound, and you check your reflection in the hot food trays to make sure you're having a good hair day.

    B. You hope he won't take too long deciding what he wants to eat — you're starving.

    C. You cross your fingers and hope he's in at least one of your classes!

"You know it's A, Felicia," Rachel said. "Admit it. I've seen you fix your hair when there's someone cute in line."

"We'll have to take your word for it, Rachel," Marilyn teased.

"You're the only one in Felicia's lunch period," Carolyn added.

"A it is," I said, clicking the mouse before Felicia could even answer.

3. Do you believe in love at first sight?

A. Yes, but it's never happened to me.
B. Oh, yes, it definitely exists — and it rocks!
C. That only happens in the movies and on soap operas.

"I think A," Felicia said. "I *totally* believe love at first sight exists out there. It's just that we're too young to actually be in love at all. We're only old enough to be in like."

"The movies and TV shows had to get the idea of love at first sight from somewhere," Liza pointed out. "The people who write the scripts must have experienced it."

No arguing with that. "Okay, A again," I clicked on the letter A and a moment later the next question popped up. "Okay, how about this one?" I continued.

4. What do you think about when you go shopping?

A. I want an outfit that fits comfortably and isn't too hard to put together.
B. I definitely need something to make me stand out from the crowd.
C. I am going to find a sweater that's his favorite color.

"It's A," Felicia said. "I totally go for comfort. I'm always doing sports so I need good sneakers, and pants I can run in."

"Yeah, but you are always pointing out things Josh has, or looks good in," Rachel pointed out.

"I am not," Felicia insisted.

"Sure you are," I told her. "Like last time we went to the mall, and you saw that leather jacket in the window. You said Josh would look really adorable in it."

Felicia blushed. "Okay. It's between A and C," Felicia admitted.

"I can only click one," I told her.

"Make it A. I don't always think about Josh when I'm shopping. Just sometimes."

"A it is," I agreed. "Next question."

5. What's scribbled all over the pages of your notebook?

A. A big heart with my name and his inside. True love 4-ever!
B. Puppies, kittens, and flowers
C. The times for the TV shows that have the cutest stars

"C," Felicia admitted. "I schedule my homework around when my favorite shows are on."

We all giggled, but no one made fun of her. Most of us scheduled our homework around our favorite shows, too.

"C it is," I said, clicking the button.

Okay, now it's time to scan your answers, total up your points and find out where you fall on the Boy Crazy Meter!

1. A. 1 point   B. 2 points   C. 3 points
2. A. 3 points   B. 1 point   C. 2 points
3. A. 2 points   B. 3 points   C. 1 point
4. A. 1 point   B. 2 points   C. 3 points
5. A. 3 points   B. 1 point   C. 2 points

A moment later, Felicia's total popped up on the screen. "You have 11 points," I read out loud.

"What does that mean?" Felicia asked.

4–7 points: You are definitely not boy crazy. In fact, you barely seem to notice that there are guys around. You might want to introduce yourself to a few — boys can be fun friends.

8–11 points: Congratulations! You've been able to walk that fine line between a healthy interest in guys (especially the cute ones!) and an absolute obsession. You're also playing it smart — guys are more likely to go for a girl who plays it cool than one who drools whenever they walk by!

12–15 points: You are out of control, girl! You've got boys on the brain — and little else. It's time to spend some more time with your girlfriends, and experience the joys of a little female bonding. Remember, boyfriends may come and go, but your girlfriends have always got your back!

"See, I'm not boy crazy!" Felicia declared triumphantly. "I told you so."

"You're awfully close, though," Liza pointed out thoughtfully. "You were at the high end of the scale."

"Yeah," Sam agreed. "If you'd just said that you think about Josh when you're shopping, you would have been out of control."

"But I don't," Felicia insisted. "And I'm not boy crazy. At least not all of the time." She looked knowingly at Sam. "And anyway, you should talk. What about how crazy you were about Jeffrey?"

"Oh, I'm over him," Sam told her. "I've moved on."

"Oh, yeah?" Marilyn asked excitedly.

"To whom?" Carolyn wondered.

Sam grinned and reached into her overnight bag. "To *him*!" she exclaimed, pulling out a picture she'd cut from a magazine. "Isn't he amazing?"

I had to admit, the guy was cute. But he looked like he was 16 or 17 years old! "Who is he?" I asked her.

Sam shrugged. "I have no idea. He's a model or an actor or something. He's in all the magazine adverts for this jeans company. I'm going to cover my binder with pictures of him so I can stare at his face all day long."

I laughed. Felicia was right. She wasn't the only one in the room who was boy crazy. But at least this time Sam had a crush on someone who couldn't get her into any trouble.

"Hey, you guys." Suddenly Chloe's voice piped up from the corner behind my bed, and I realized she hadn't said a word during the whole quiz. That was kind of unusual for her.

"What's up, Chloe?" I asked her.

"Can someone go over this scene with me one more time?" she asked. "I think I have it completely memorized now."

"Sure, I will," Sam agreed, sliding over toward where Chloe was sitting, and taking the script from her hands.

"I really appreciate it," Chloe told her sincerely.

"No problem," Sam assured her. "Just promise me one thing."

"What?" Chloe asked.

"When you get famous, you'll introduce me to that guy in the jeans adverts!" Sam giggled.

"You got it," Chloe agreed with a grin.

We all sat back and listened as Chloe went over her lines from the piano scene. I barely breathed as I listened, hoping she didn't make a single mistake. Finally, Sam put down the papers and grinned. "That's it. Perfect," she told Chloe. "You're going to be amazing tomorrow night."

Chloe shook her head. "I'm going to be a mess."

"What are you talking about?" I asked her. "Sam just said you knew your lines perfectly."

"Yeah, but I'm exhausted. It's almost two o'clock in the morning, and I have that special rehearsal in a few hours. I'm going to have big dark circles under my eyes."

"No you won't," I promised her as I ran my cursor through a list on middleschoolsurvival.com. "Listen to this."

Lemony-Fresh Facials

It's time to steam things up. Nothing works better than a hot facial to give your skin a gorgeous natural glow. Here's how to give yourself a fantastic facial:

Start by boiling water. While the water is boiling, wash your face with soap and water, then cover your head with a towel. Ask an adult to carefully pour the boiling water into a bowl. Then add one or two drops of lemon juice. Allow the sides of the towel to hang over the bowl like a tent as you lean your face down until it is six inches from the bowl. Stay like that for no more than three minutes.

"That sounds like fun!" Sam exclaimed. "Let's try that one first thing in the morning. I've always wanted to have a facial. My mum loves getting them."

"Mine, too," I told her. "And there's more stuff we can do tomorrow morning, too. Here's a way to make sure your eyes aren't puffy or red even if you haven't had enough sleep."

"That's just what I need," Chloe told me. "Read it!"

The Eyes Have It

When you've finished your facial, it's time to soften the delicate skin around your eyes, and get rid of any telltale dark circles. To do that, carefully cut a cucumber into thin slices. Be sure to do this just before you plan to use the slices so they don't dry out. Now lay flat on a bed or on the floor. Place one cucumber slice on each eye. (Be sure to keep your eyes closed!) Rest like that for five minutes. Then remove the cucumber slices. You're sure to look as though you've had a full night of sleep, even if you've been up all night.

"See?" I said, after I read the whole thing out loud. "All we need is hot water, lemon juice, and cucumber slices, and you'll be gorgeous tomorrow!"

"Either that," Chloe said with a laugh as she climbed into her sleeping bag, "or I'm going to smell like a salad."

Chapter
TEN

AS I STOOD in the wings of the school theater and heard the applause, I let out a huge sigh of relief. It felt like I hadn't breathed once since the show began. That's how nervous I was for Chloe. But here it was, over, and Chloe had done a great job. She hadn't missed one line or walked into a single piece of scenery. And better than that, she'd been funny. Really funny!

I peeked out from behind the curtain to get a good glimpse of the audience. Everyone was smiling and cheering. Everyone but the Pops, that is. They just sat there in their seats. They were really bummed that Chloe had done so well. Even they wouldn't be able to find anything to make fun of in her performance. I guess that kind of ruined the whole night for them.

But it really made ours. We were all incredibly proud of Chloe — especially because we knew how hard she'd worked.

"She did it!" Liza squealed with delight. "She really did it."

"I have to admit I had my doubts," Sam added. "I mean, learning all those lines in one night . . ."

"You guys, thank you!" Chloe exclaimed, running

backstage as the curtain closed. "I mean, thank you so much! I could never have done this without you, never!"

"We didn't do so much," I assured her. "You're the one who had to memorize everything. We were just there for moral support."

"Nope," Chloe shook her head so hard her black wig tilted slightly on her forehead. "This was a total team effort. We're all sharing in this success!"

"Okay," I agreed with a grin. "Do we all get to share in a celebratory ice cream, too?"

"Of course," Chloe assured me. "My parents are waiting in the lobby for us. I just have to change out of my costume."

As Chloe headed off into the dressing room, I looked over at Liza. "Okay, so you're our next project," I told her.

"Me?" She sounded confused.

"Oh, yeah," I said. "You have the state history bee coming up in a few weeks. I think we'll have to have at least three sleepovers to get you ready for that."

Liza giggled. "You ever wonder why they call them sleepovers?" she asked. "I mean, no one ever sleeps."

"Don't worry. I'll be sure to have plenty of cucumbers handy," I joked.

"So, Chloe, tell us how it feels to be the star of Joyce Kilmer Middle School?" Marc asked, pointing his camera in her direction as we all sat together at a big table at Richmann's Ice Cream Parlor.

Chloe stood and lifted her ice cream sundae in front of her as though it were an award. "I'd like to thank all the little people who made this evening possible."

Felicia stood up tall, so that she was every one of her five foot three inches. She looked down on the top of Chloe's head. "Who are you calling little?" she teased.

Chloe giggled. "Not you."

"Uh, Chloe," I interrupted. "I think your trophy is dripping onto your shirt."

Chloe looked down. Sure enough, the strawberry ice cream and nuts had started making their way onto her blue "Drama Queen" T-shirt. "I guess it's time to end my acceptance speech," she shrugged, sitting down and scooping up a spoonful of ice cream and hot fudge.

"Maybe they should try dripping ice cream on movie stars when their speeches go on too long at awards shows," Sam suggested. "That would get them off the stage really quickly!"

"Speaking of ice cream," Rachel interrupted. "Do you guys know how astronauts eat their ice cream?"

"No. How?" Sam asked.

"In floats!" Rachel told her. She laughed at her own joke.

Everyone else just groaned. "Okay, that one was just painful," Felicia teased her.

As I looked around the table, I realized that I was the happiest I'd been in a long time. Sure, I'd lost my old best friend, but I'd gained a whole lot of new ones. And maybe we weren't the trendsetters at our school, but we really liked one another. And we were there for one another when things were tough, which was more important than having the best clothes, or wearing the perfect makeup all the time. The Pops would probably never understand that. But I sure did. Because thanks to my friends, I knew for sure that no matter what problems I might face, surviving middle school was going to be a blast!

How Honest are You?

Is honesty your policy? Or is "liar, liar pants on fire" more your motto? There's only one way to find out the truth about yourself. You've gotta take the quiz:

1. **You're walking down the aisle at the pharmacy when your backpack hits a bottle of nail polish. The bottle falls to the floor, shatters, and leaves blood red polish all over the place. The thing is, no one saw you hit the bottle. What's your next move?**

   A. Walk out of the store as fast as you can before someone figures out what happened.

   B. Find the store manager and tell her you broke the nail polish — and offer to pay for it and help clean up.

   C. Tell the store manager there's nail polish all over the floor in aisle 3 — but never admit it's your fault.

2. **You promised your BFF you'd go to the mall with her on Saturday night to help her pick out a cute pair of leather boots. But at the last minute, another friend calls with two tickets to a sold out concert you've been dying to see. How do you handle this one?**

A. Hit the mall with your BFF as you originally planned. You'll just have to hear that hot band on your iPod.

B. Call your BFF, explain about the concert and ask to change your shopping plans to Sunday afternoon.

C. Call your BFF and tell her you have to go see your grandparents — then go to the concert.

3. **As you and your friend are leaving your favorite ice-cream parlor, you realize the cashier handed you an extra five-dollar bill with your change. What's your response?**

A. Pocket the cash. It's the cashier's fault, after all.

B. Go back and return the money to the cashier.

C. Split your newfound cash 50-50 with your pal.

4. **You borrow a shirt from a pal, and accidentally get a small tear in the sleeve. What do you do?**

A. Use your allowance money to replace her old shirt with a brand new one. Now she never has to know you were irresponsible with her clothes.

B. Return it and never mention the rip. It's so tiny she may not notice it at first. By the time she does, she'll think she tore it herself.

C. Admit what happened, apologize, and offer to replace the torn shirt with a new shirt of her choice.

Okay, time to add up your score!

1. A. 3 points   B. 1 point   C. 2 points
2. A. 1 point   B. 2 points C. 3 points
3. A. 3 points   B. 1 point   C. 2 points
4. A. 2 points   B. 3 points C. 1 point

4-5 points: You are incredibly honest and trustworthy. In fact, your score is so amazing that we just have to ask — did you answer all of these questions honestly?

6-9 points: This is where most people fall on the honesty scale. For the most part, you're an honest human being, but every now and then, you fudge or fib a little bit. Sometimes, that's okay though — especially when you're trying to spare people you care about.

10-12 points: Uh-oh! Lying may have become a way of life for you. You might want to take a closer look at why you lie — and then try the truth for a change. You may be surprised at how well things turn out.

NANCY KRULIK HAS WRITTEN more than 150 books for children and young adults, including three *New York Times* bestsellers. She is the author of the popular Katie Kazoo Switcheroo series and is also well known as a biographer of Hollywood's hottest young stars. Her knowledge of the details of celebrities' lives has made her a desired guest on several entertainment shows on the E! network as well as on *Extra* and *Access Hollywood.* Nancy lives in Manhattan with her husband, composer Daniel Burwasser, their two children, Ian and Amanda, and a crazy cocker spaniel named Pepper.

Will Jenny survive middle school?

Jenny's happy to start school with her best friend, Addie, by her side. But Addie has other plans—and they don't include Jenny!

Addie's running for class president and there's only one way to stop her—Jenny will have to run against her.

The school gossip column is revealing everyone's secrets! Can Jenny figure out who the snitch is?

■SCHOLASTIC

www.middleschoolsurvival.com

SCHOOLBLST

Log on to my favorite Web site!

www.middleschoolsurvival.com

You'll find:
- Cool Polls and Quizzes
- Tips and Advice
- Message Boards
- And Everything Else You Need to Survive Middle School!